Written by Kim Widdis

illustrated by: Kae Parker

Balboa Press books may be ordered through booksellers or by contacting:

Balboa Press
A Division of Hay House
1663 Liberty Drive
Bloomington, IN 47403
www.balboapress.com
844-682-1282

ISBN: 978-1-9822-7193-0 (sc)
ISBN: 978-1-9822-7328-6 (e)

Print information available on the last page.

Balboa Press rev. date: 08/26/2021

BALBOA.PRESS

Edna loves visiting her Aunt Ruth for sleepovers. When she stays over, they talk to the moon until Edna slips into sleep.

Edna tells the moon about all her fondest fantasies and grandest adventures.

She tells the moon about the beautiful crafts she made at school and the difficult spelling tests she didn't do very well on.

1

Aunt Ruth holds Edna in her arms and listens to Edna catch up with her darling friend the moon for as long as it takes little Edna to feel all talked out.

Edna always has the best sleep and most delightful dreams after a long talk with the moon through Aunt Ruth's window.

Most days Edna has many happy
tales to tell the moon.

But sometimes, when she's had a hard day or if she's lost one of her favorite toys, she just wants to tell the moon she's sad. This usually helps Edna feel much better.

One day Edna has her hardest day ever.
Edna's dad dies and she is really sad that
she won't be able to see him anymore.

All Edna can think to do is go to Aunt Ruth's
for a sleepover so she can speak to the moon.
Edna wants very badly to let all her feelings
drift up to the moon through her words so that
she can sleep and dream of pleasant things.

Edna asks her mom to call Aunt Ruth so that she can sleep over, and when Aunt Ruth picks up the phone she listens closely to Edna's sad words. Aunt Ruth tells Edna, "You just stay put my dear, I'll be right over. I have something to show you." Edna waits for Aunt Ruth.

When Aunt Ruth arrives, she scoops Edna up in her arms and takes her to Edna's bedroom window. She pulls open the curtain and says, "The moon will always be in your sky whether it's night or day, in my house or yours. Between the moon in the sky and your father in your heart you will always have someone to talk to."

13

That night Aunt Ruth stays at Edna's house and holds her while Edna speaks to the moon.

Edna tells the moon that she feels angry that she doesn't get to see her dad anymore. Edna tells the moon that she feels sad because her house is quiet without her dad's voice. Edna tells the moon that she is worried her mom will feel lonely with her dad gone.

The moon listens and so does Aunt Ruth and after a long while, Edna feels tired and a little less sad. She slips into a deep sleep until morning.

The next day at school Edna starts to feel
very sad and finds it hard to pay attention.
Edna thinks about what Aunt Ruth said,

"Between the moon in the sky and your father in your
heart, you will always have someone to talk to."

Edna asks her teacher if she can be excused and goes out into the hallway. She takes a moment to speak to the moon and lets out her sadness. There is no window, and she can't see the moon, but she knows she is never alone.

23

Printed in the United States
by Baker & Taylor Publisher Services